This Faber book belongs to

- -

For the
Mi'kmaq people, for whom
there is a gateway between this world
and the spirit world. J. A.

For my Nana. J. C-T.

First published in 2017 by Faber and Faber Limited
Bloomsbury House 74–77 Great Russell Street London WC1B 3DA

Designed by Faber and Faber

Printed in Europe

All rights reserved

Text © John Agard, 2017
Illustrations © Jessica Courtney-Tickle, 2017

A CIP record for this book is available from the British Library

PB ISBN 978–0571–32416–3

2 4 6 8 10 9 7 5 3 1

MIX
Paper from
responsible sources
FSC
www.fsc.org FSC® C022612

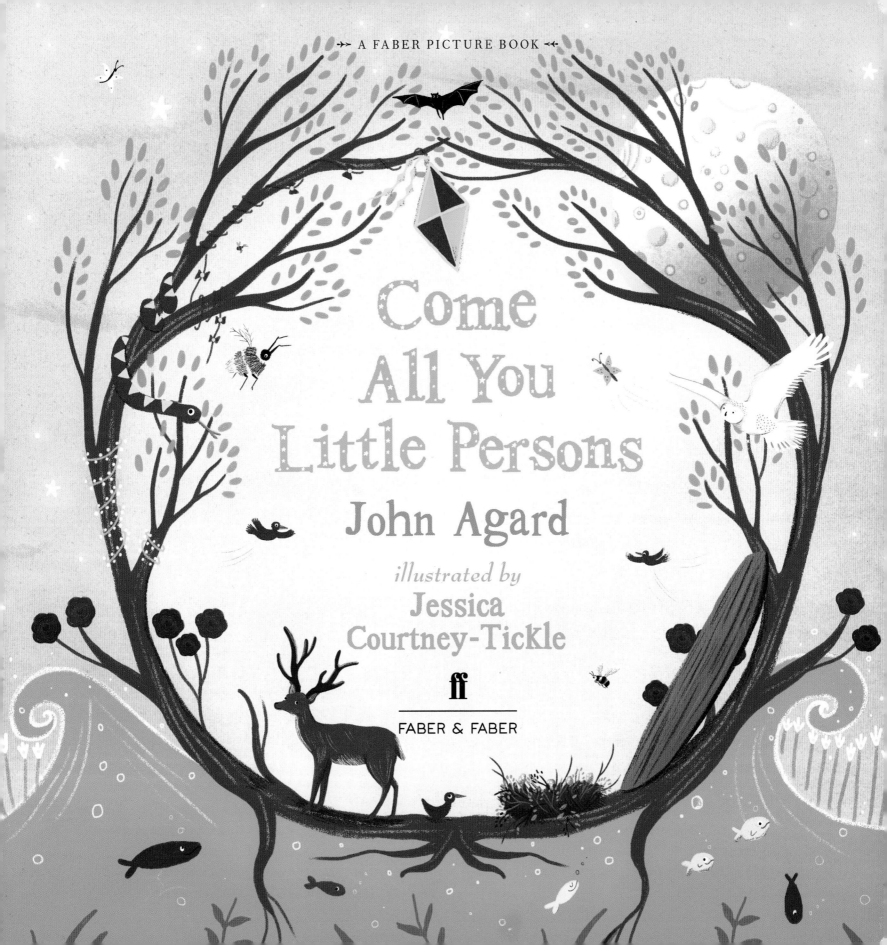

Come All You Little Persons

John Agard

illustrated by

Jessica Courtney-Tickle

ff

FABER & FABER

From above earth, from above sky,
from below earth, from under water,
come all you little persons
come exactly as you are.

Come little bird-person in feathered cape.

Come little fish-person
in blouse of scales.

Come little tree-person
in robe of leaves.

Come little snake-person
in sheddable sleeves.

Come little wave-person
in shirt made of spray.

Come little mouse-person
in Sunday-best grey.

Come little moon-person
in apron that shines.

Come little bat-person
in cape of night-time.

Come little star-person
in five-pointed crown.

Come little wind-person
in invisible gown.

Come little sun-person
in dazzling tiara.

Come little bee-person
in fairylight attire.

You too little stone-person
in rags of molten fire.

Come all you little persons
come join the dance of
Earth's guests.

Just follow your heart-song
when next it calls.
Planet Earth has room for the
footsteps of all.